When I Was Built

Written and Illustrated by

JENNIFER THERMES

Henry Holt and Company
New York

Henry Holt and Company, LLC
Publishers since 1866
115 West 18th Street
New York, New York 10011

Henry Holt is a registered trademark
of Henry Holt and Company, LLC

Published in Canada by Fitzhenry & Whiteside Ltd.,
195 Allstate Parkway, Markham, Ontario L3R 4T8.

Library of Congress Cataloging-in-Publication Data
Thermes, Jennifer.
When I was built / written and illustrated by Jennifer Thermes.
Summary: An old house describes the way of life of the family that built it
many years ago, and that of the one living in it today.
[1. Dwellings—Fiction. 2. Family life—Fiction.] I. Title.
PZ7.T35238 Wh 2001 [E]—dc21 00-44854

ISBN 0-8050-6532-6
First Edition—2001
Printed in the United States of America on acid-free paper. ∞
1 3 5 7 9 10 8 6 4 2

The artist used pen and ink and watercolor
on bristol board to create the illustrations for this book.

For Jeremy and Emily
and all future children who live in this home—
an old house is a wise teacher.

I AM AN OLD HOUSE. I live here, next to the side of the road, where a farmer named Fairchild built me a long time ago. He built me small and strong, and through the years I've had many children grow up within my walls. Today, I still stand proud, with the Gray family living inside. I watch the world pass by, and sometimes think about the way things were when I was first built.

Today, big houses surround me, up and down my street.

When I was built, the Fairchilds were the only people around for miles and miles.

Today, I hear the rumble of big machines and power tools that make it easier for people to build large houses.

When I was built, farmer Fairchild gathered large stones for my foundation with his horse and plow from the rocky field behind me. He cut wood for my beams with his ax in a nearby grove of trees. Friends came to help raise my walls, and then to celebrate.

Today, I jump when the big steel furnace in my basement turns on with a boom. The blowing hot air keeps Elizabeth and Peter Gray warm, even in February.

When I was built, my rooms were made small and my ceilings low to hold in heat from the fireplace, which warmed the Fairchilds through the long winter.

Today, I have a bathroom built under the slope of my roof. Hot and cold water runs through copper pipes and fills my bathtub and toilet.

When I was built, I watched Maggie and Andrew Fairchild walk across the back field to my outhouse to use the bathroom. They carried buckets of well water to heat over my hearth at wash-time, even in the middle of winter. In those days, people didn't usually take a bath more than once or twice a month.

Today, the Grays sometimes eat at pizza parlors and fast-food restaurants. They shop at the grocery store in town, which sells food from all over the world. Cooking a meal is quick and easy with the help of the electric stove and microwave oven in my new kitchen.

When I was built, the Fairchilds ate vegetables grown in their garden and meat from animals raised on their farm. I smelled stews cooking in iron pots over my hearth and crusty bread baking in my beehive oven.

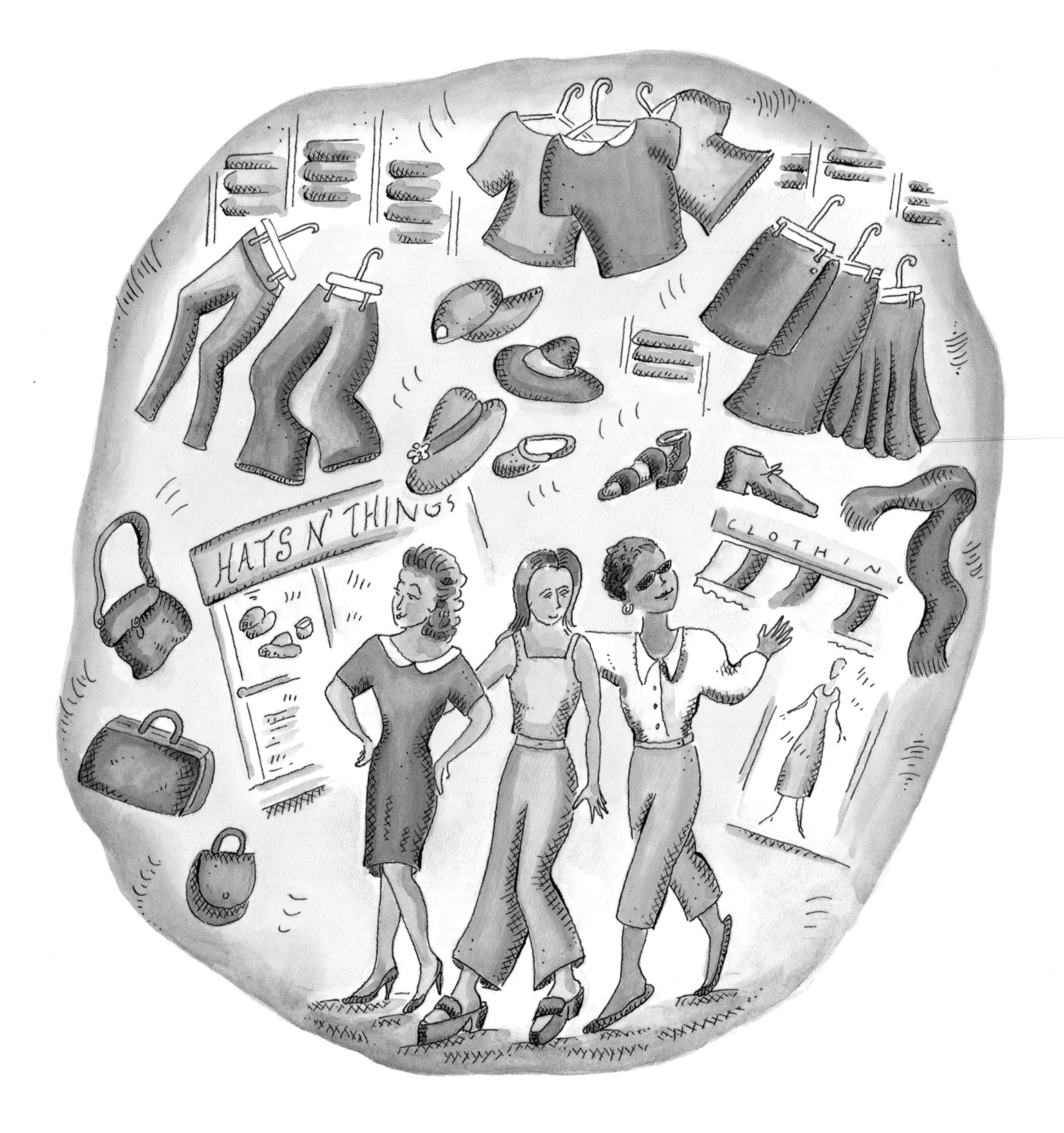

Today, malls and stores have pants, shirts, dresses, coats, hats, and skirts in hundreds of styles and colors.

When I was built, there were few shops in which to buy clothes. I watched Maggie Fairchild and her mother make their own dresses from sheep wool and flax spun into yarn.

Today, there are electric lamps and television
sets that light up the night with noise and chatter.

When I was built, I listened as the Fairchilds passed quiet evenings together, talking or reading or telling stories, their faces aglow in the flickering candles.

Today, I hear telephones jangle wildly. The Grays' fax machine hums and their computer bleeps with urgent information from minute to minute.

When I was built, the Fairchilds sent their news in letters, delivered by a man on horseback. It could take weeks for messages to reach faraway friends.

Today, I see cars and trucks race past my front door on the slick black pavement.

When I was built, the road was just a rutted dirt path. I followed the slow clip-clop rhythm of a passing horse and wagon, and the quiet footsteps of a walking neighbor.

Today, I feel airplanes roar over my roof and rattle my old windowpanes. They leave behind chalky patterns that crisscross the sky, as their passengers travel all over the world in hours.

When I was built, the world was my front yard, and people stayed closer to home. I listened to the soft chattering of crickets and to Maggie and Andrew Fairchild laughing when they chased birds and dragonflies nesting around my walls.

Today, I watch the Gray children play and swing on my backyard gymset in the afternoon when all their homework is done. Sometimes they catch the old croaking frogs in my pond.

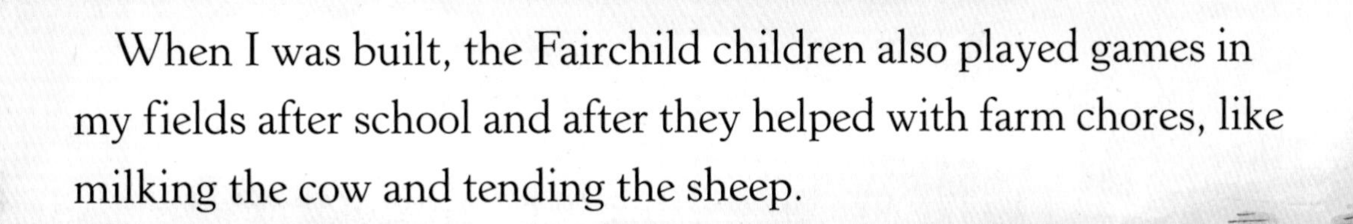

When I was built, the Fairchild children also played games in my fields after school and after they helped with farm chores, like milking the cow and tending the sheep.

When I was built, I felt the footsteps of Maggie and Andrew Fairchild thumping up and down my steep staircase, chasing each other through my rooms. They rested beside my warm fireplace, and I listened to their whispered dreams when they went to sleep in the evening. I saw them gaze out my windows and wonder about what changes the future would bring.

And today, Elizabeth and Peter Gray do the same.

LOWER MERION LIBRARY SYSTEM
30043002310872